SHAPE
SHIFT

Joyce Hesselberth

Christy Ottaviano Books
Henry Holt and Company · New York

The Shapes

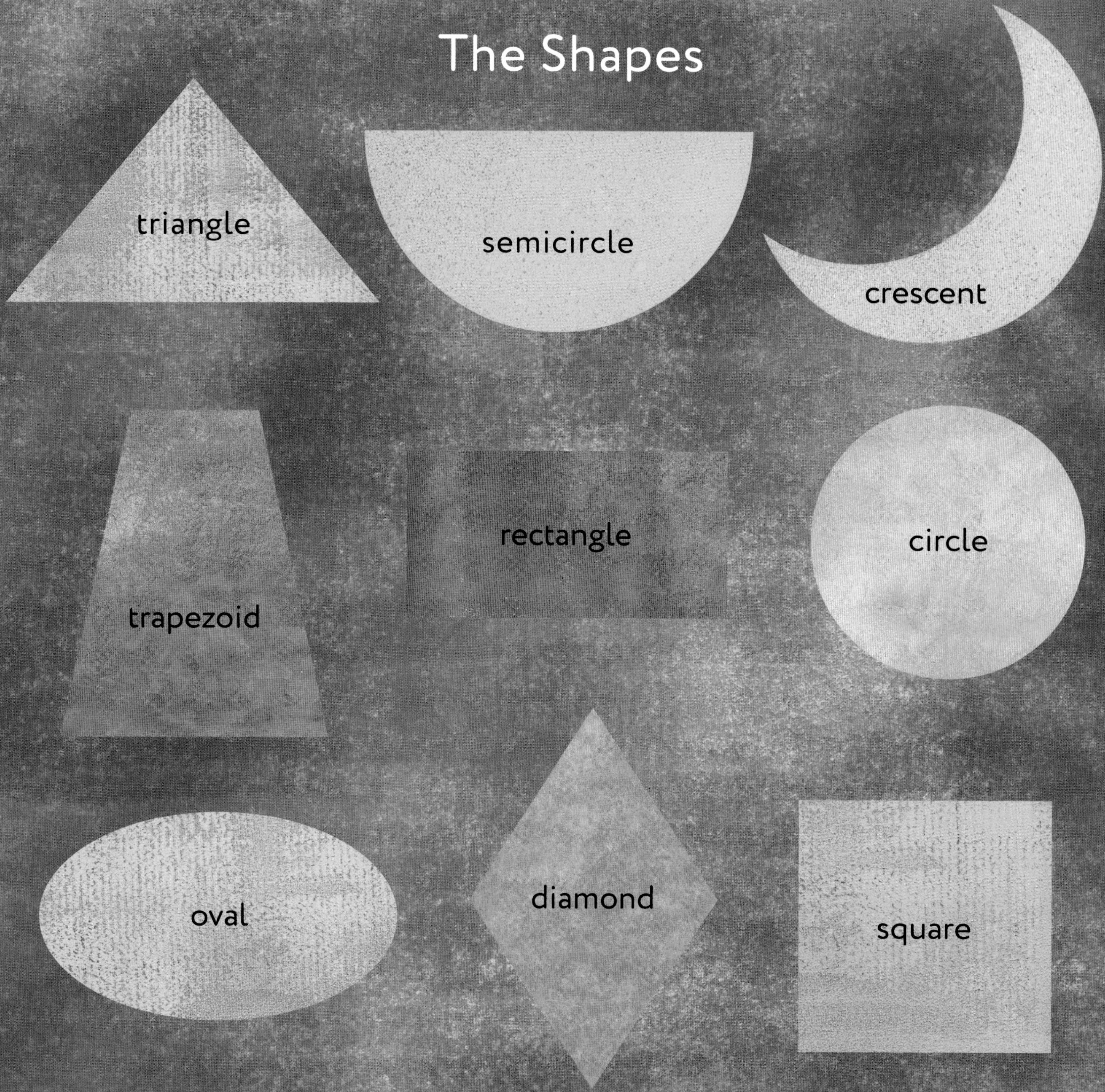

triangle

semicircle

crescent

trapezoid

rectangle

circle

oval

diamond

square

Look around. What shapes do you see?

I see a rectangle house with a trapezoid roof. I see a triangle tree.
Shapes are all around us. Once you know how to find them,
you can use shapes to make anything you'd like.

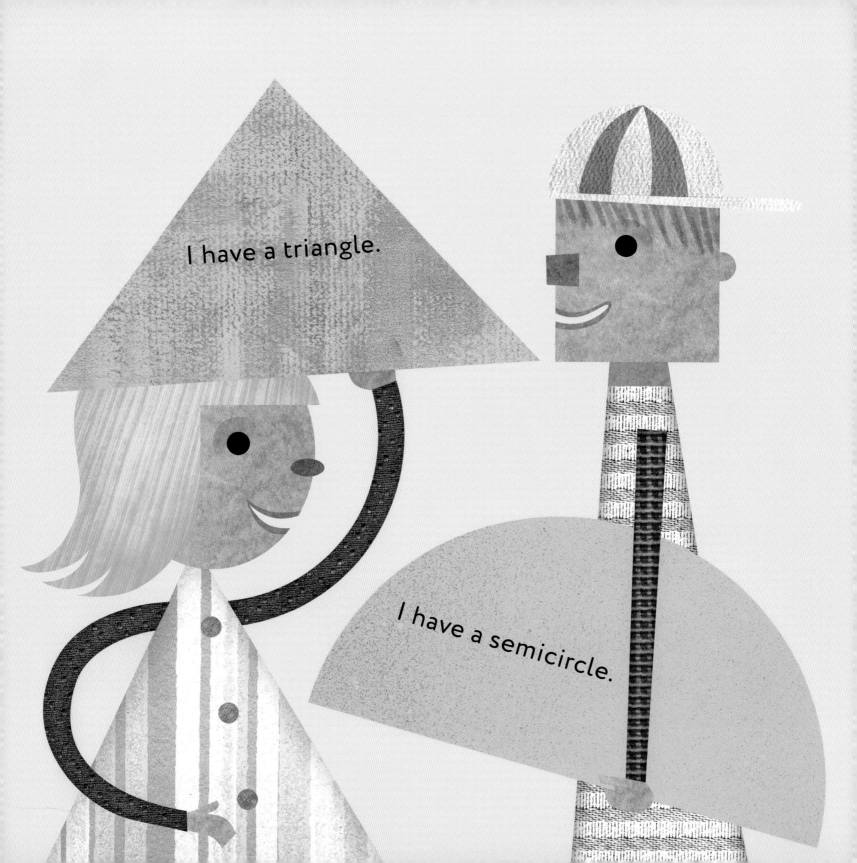

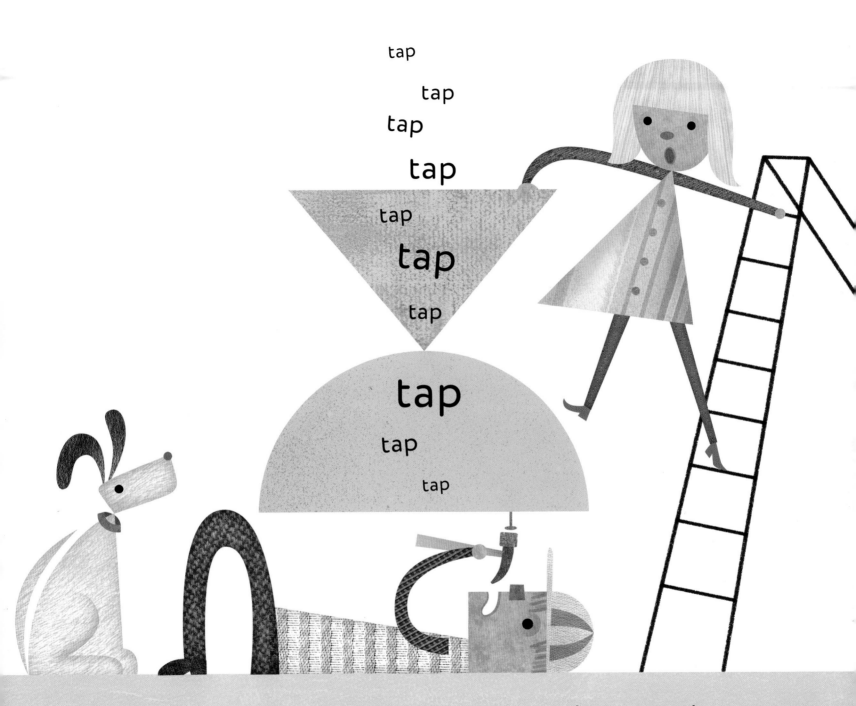

tap
tap
tap
tap
tap
tap
tap
tap
tap
tap

Let's put our shapes together and
see what we can make!

I see a ballerina,

twirling,

spinning,

gliding,

floating

across

a stage.

I see an elephant, flying high with a thousand balloons.

Up,

up,

and

away!

Arrgghhh...

What is it?

I see an angry bull, ready to charge.

Why are you so grumpy, Mr. Bull?

I see a slippery fish, jumping in the waves.

Splish! Splash! Swish! Jump, little fish!

What do you see?

I see a lady with a fancy hat.

Head held
high, she
passes by.
I wonder
where she's
going.

I see a super car zooming down the road.

Zooma-zoom,

zoom-zooma,

zoooooooommm!

Last game, and this one's tricky.
Let's try to solve it together!

Do you know what it is?

We see a clown. Upside down.
Silly clown! How long can he stay that way?

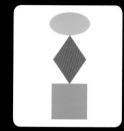

1 2 3 4 5 6

7 8 9 10...

We see watermelon, sweet and crisp . . .

Now it's your turn.
Here are some more shapes.

What do you see?

For Mom and Dad

Henry Holt and Company, LLC
Publishers since 1866
175 Fifth Avenue
New York, New York 10010
mackids.com

Library of Congress Cataloging-in-Publication Data
Hesselberth, Joyce, author, illustrator.
Shape shift / Joyce Hesselberth.—First edition.
pages   cm
Summary: "Round, curvy, pointy, or straight, shapes are all around us. With illustrations that highlight shapes in all their forms,
this book reinforces the identification of circles, squares, crescents, diamonds, triangles, rectangles, trapezoids, and
ovals while encouraging kids to pair shapes together to make new forms"—Provided by publisher.
ISBN 978-1-62779-057-4 (hardback)
[1. Shape—Fiction. 2. Imagination—Fiction.] I. Title.
PZ7.1.H53Sh 2016   [E]—dc23   2015003032

Henry Holt books may be purchased for business or promotional use.
For information on bulk purchases, please contact the Macmillan Corporate and
Premium Sales Department at (800) 221-7945 x5442 or by e-mail at specialmarkets@macmillan.com.

First Edition—2016
The artist used mixed media and digital paint to create the illustrations in this book.
Printed in China by Macmillan Production Asia Ltd., Kowloon Bay, Hong Kong (vendor code: 10)

1 3 5 7 9 10 8 6 4 2